Phoney Bone

Page 55

The Road to Barrelhaven

Page 77

Trapped

Page 99

Phoney's Inferno

Page 121

The Complete Bone Adventures ©1993 Jeff

P.O. Box 1583, Los Gatos, CA 95031-1583. Any similarity between characters/institutions in this work to actual characters/institutions is unintended. BONE is a trademark of Jeff Smith. All Rights reserved. Printed in Canada ISBN 0-9636609-0-X

D1473783

THIS BOOK IS
FOR
VIJAYA

FOREWORD

By Will Eisner

For me, perhaps one of the most exciting happenings in the world of comic books has been the opportunity to self-publish by young cartoonists. I find it so important to the creative health of the comics medium because it has yielded such a rich harvest. Out of the recent crop has come a most promising and refreshing new work called BONE -- Jeff Smith's tale of a hilarious and charming creature lost in a fairy tale world.

Starting from where Walt Kelly left off, Smith manages to soar into his own orbit with an improbable, impertinent creature who lives comfortably in the company of the real people and animals that inhabit the Valley.

The genius of BONE is that its author skillfully cloaks the naked pixie with reality and before we know it...he is us.

Despite the bare bones (oops!) style used to render Bone, the supporting cast reveals Smith's competence as a draftsman. In all, he infuses the work with animation and fantasy. He is adept at adding realistic rendered animals and backgrounds into the mix.

I felt, when I first read BONE (it was an easy and fun read!), that what I was looking at was a comic with potential. After a half a dozen issues, I was sure of it.

I expect this collection will reaffirm that all is well in Boneville, and its future is bright. It's a great place to visit.

Will Eisner

5

DON'T GET HIM STARTED.

THEY CAN'T **DO** THIS TO **ME!** YOU CAN'T DO ANYTHING TO A **RICH** PERSON THAT HE DOESN'T **WANT!**

GASP! OH! TH' HORRIBLE INJUSTICE OF IT ALL! I'M STILL **REELING** WITH **SHOCK!!**

I'M A RESPECTED COMMUNITY **LEADER!** A **SHINING PILLAR** OF **MORAL STRENGTH!**

.... SO A COUPLE OF SHADY **BUSINESS** DEALS WENT SOUR... IS **THAT** ANY REASON TO RUN TH' MOST **BELOVED BONE** IN BONEVILLE OUT ON A **RAIL?!**

YES.

BELOVED? TH' MAYOR DECLARED A SCHOOL **HOLIDAY** JUST SO TH' KIDS COULD COME AND THROW **ROCKS** AT YOU!

INGRATES! OH, THEY'LL **RUE** TH' DAY THEY CHASED **PHONCIBLE P. BONE** OUTTA THEIR CRUMMY OL' TOWN!

≷ SNIFF! ≷

NOW, NOW, LITTLE BUCKAROO! DON'T BE **SAD!** IT'S A BEAUTIFUL DAY! THERE'S NOT A **CLOUD** IN TH' SKY!

7

8

9

11

YEEEE! I CAN'T BELIEVE I WASN'T JUST KILLED!

PHONEY! SMILEY! GO BACK! DON'T COME THIS WAY! IT'S A CLIFF!

....MAYBE THEY'RE ALREADY DOWN HERE!

PHONEY BONE! SMILEY!

HEY!

HEY, GUYS! I'M DOWN IN THIS GULLEY! CAN YOU HEAR ME?!!

PHONEY--❋
SAY! THERE'S THAT MAP!

HUH! I WONDER IF THIS REALLY **IS** A MAP OF THAT MOUNTAIN RANGE...MAYBE I BETTER HANG ON TO IT!

I MIGHT NEED IT TO SAVE PHONEY BONE...

...AGAIN!

HMMF.

I'M ALWAYS GETTIN' HIM OUTTA TROUBLE!

WELL, COUSIN OR NOT... WHEN WE GET BACK TO BONEVILLE, PHONEY'S GONNA HAVE TO FACE THE MUSIC BY **HIMSELF!**

I'VE **HAD** IT! FROM NOW ON, HE CAN OUT RUN ANGRY **MOBS,** AN' FALL OFF **CLIFFS** WITHOUT **MY** HELP!

WHAT KIND OF A **PATSY** DOES HE **TAKE** ME FOR ?! URNF !

IT'S ALWAYS: "FONE BONE, YOU GOTTA **SAVE** ME !" OR: "FONE BONE, YOU GOTTA **HELP** ME !"

WHY, I OUGHTA--

HEY! HOW'D I GET SO CLOSE TO THE **MOUNTAINS?!**

WHERE **IS** EVERYBODY? WHERE'S TH' **LOCUSTS?!**

NO WAY! I CLIMBED UP THE **WRONG SIDE!** **PHONEY! HELP!! YOU GOTTA SAVE ME !!**

14

HUH
HUH
HUH

HUFF!

WHERE TH' HECK **ARE** THOSE GUYS? WE'RE GOIN' STRAIGHT INTO TH' MOUNTAINS!

I HOPE I CATCH UP TO 'EM BEFORE IT GETS DARK....

THE **LAST** THING I WANT TO DO IS SPEND THE NIGHT OUT HERE BY MYSELF!

...OF COURSE, AFTER A DAY LIKE **TODAY**, IT'S HARD TO IMAGINE THAT ANYTHING **WORSE** COULD HAPPEN...

YAWN!

OOG....
I MUST'VE
FALLEN
ASLEEP.

WHERE
AM I?

YOU
AWAKE?

HUH?
WHO'S
THERE?

YOU
GOT A
LIGHT?

SMILEY?
IS THAT
YOU?

OH, BOY, AM
I GLAD TO
SEE YOU!
HOLD ON, I'VE
GOT A MATCH
IN MY BAG,
HERE!

SKRITCH

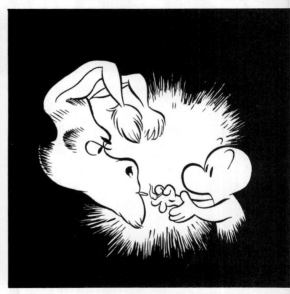

AAAH!

THANKS FOR TH' LIGHT.

DON'T MENTION IT!

SKRITCH

HELLO?

HELLO?

OH, MAN! I GOTTA QUIT GOIN' TO SLEEP ON AN **EMPTY STOMACH!**

OH, **MAN!** THIS AIN'T GONNA **CUT IT!**

I ACTUALLY THOUGHT THIS MAP WOULD TAKE ME THROUGH TH' MOUNTAINS TO THIS WATERFALL ON HERE...

...BUT IF THIS THING WERE **REAL,** I WOULD'VE COME TO TH' **PASS** BY **NOW!** ERRR! I'M SO **STUPID!** I BET THIS MAP WAS JUST ONE OF SMILEY'S **PRANKS** --AND I **FELL** FOR IT!

AND TO TOP IT **OFF,** I HAVEN'T SEEN ANY MORE **CIGAR BUTTS** ALL DAY... **HOW** DO I GET MYSELF **INTO** THESE THINGS?

OH, WELL... I'LL FIND THOSE GUYS **SOONER** OR LATER... IF I DON'T DIE OF THIRST...

UNTIL **THEN,** I JUST GOTTA KEEP MOVIN'! KEEP...

COOL.

I MADE IT!

THAT STUPID MAP WAS **RIGHT!** YESSIREE, **BOB!** THERE'S WATER ON TH' MENU **TONIGHT!**

I COULD **KISS** SMILEY BONE FOR FINDING THAT MAP!

I MIGHT EVEN KISS **PHONEY** RIGHT BEFORE I STRANGLE HIM!

BUT YOU BETTER FIND IT--**FAST**! IT'S AUTUMN NOW, AN' WINTER STRIKES **QUICK** IN THESE PARTS... AN' WHEN IT DOES, **NOBODY** CAN GET THROUGH THOSE MOUNTAINS...

...IN **OR** OUT!

SO I SUGGEST YOU MAKE YOUR VISIT HERE A **SHORT** ONE, OR YOU'LL BE STUCK FOR TH' WINTER. AN' **I** DON'T THINK YOU WANNA **DO** THAT!

NO. DEFINITELY NOT.

GOOD. I'LL LET YA GO FOR **NOW**, SINCE TED SEEMS TO LIKE YA OKAY... BUT DON'T FERGET!

NO DAWDLIN'!

THANK YOU FOR NOT HITTING ME.

DON'T WORRY 'BOUT HIM... HE'S ACTUAL A REAL NICE GUY!

WELL... NOW WE GOTTA FIGGER OUT WHAT TA **DO** WITH YA... SAY! I KNOW! I'LL TAKE YA TO SEE THORN! C'MON! WHAT'S YER **NAME**, MISTER?

FONE BONE. SO WHO'S THIS THORN? HE'S NOT ANOTHER **BIG BUG**, IS HE?

HO, HO! **NO**! THORN KNOWS JES' ABOUT EVER'THIN' IN TH' **WHOLE WORLD**!

BUT, LISTEN, BONE! BIG BROTHER WAS RIGHT ABOUT WINTER! SHE HITS **FAST**! 'N' IF YOU WANTS TA GIT HOME, YOU GOTTA DO IT BEFORE SHE **SNOWS**!

DON'T WORRY! I'M JUST GONNA FIND MY COUSINS, AN' THEN I'M **OUTTA HERE**!

24

WHERE CAN I GET SOMETHING TO DRINK? I'M DYIN' OF THIRST!

WE CAN STOP BY TH' **BARRELHAVEN**! THEY BREWS TH' BEST STUFF AROUN'!

eh?

COMRADE! WE ARE ABOUT TO **FEAST!** QUICK! GET YOUR **FAT CARCASS** BEHIND THIS BUSH AND GET READY!

HELLO, SMALL MAMMAL.....COULD YOU STEP IN HERE FOR A MOMENT? I'VE GOT SOMETHING TO SHOW YOU....

CAN'T YOU SHOW ME OUT HERE, WHERE I'VE GOT RUNNIN' SPACE?

NO! NO! PLEASE! STEP IN HERE -- YOUR FRIEND THE DRAGON ISN'T AROUND, IS HE?

HEY, TED! WHERE YOU GOIN'?

YOU'RE ON YER **OWN** BONE!

QUICK, COMRADE! START THE COOKING FIRE!

NO. YOU CALLED ME FAT.

25

TED!

C'MON, TED! WHERE **ARE** YOU? YOU GOTTA TAKE ME TO SEE THORN!

-- I'M SORRY I CALLED YOU A **LEAF**!

WHOOOOOP! WATER! I HEAR **WATER**!!

WATER!

WATER! WATER!

WATER! MMMM **WATER**! WATER! MMMM WATER! WATER! MMMMMM MM MM OH, **MAN**!

WHAT AM I GONNA **DO**? WHAT IF I **CAN'T** FIND MY COUSINS BEFORE IT **SNOWS**? WE COULD BE **TRAPPED** HERE FOR TH' WHOLE **WINTER**!

I **GOTTA** GET OUTTA HERE! THIS FOREST IS TOO **WEIRD** FOR ME!

RUMMMMBLE

WHUMP!

CASE IN POINT.

Next: THORN

HELLO, MIZ 'POSSUM! I HAVEN'T SEEN **YOU** IN A COUPLE OF MONTHS!

OH, I DON'T GET OUT OF TH' HOUSE MUCH IN **WINTER...** 'SPECIALLY WITH **YOUNGUNS!**

THESE CAN'T BE **YOUR** KIDS! THEY'RE ALL GROWN UP!

WELL, IT'S ALMOST **SPRING!** THEY SHOOT UP **FAST** THIS TIME OF YEAR! YOU BOYS REMEMBER FONE BONE?

SURE!

YEAH!

HOW YOU GUYS DOIN'?

WE'RE COOL.

WHERE'D YA GET TH' **HAT?**

YOUR MOM MADE IT FOR ME!

PRETTY DORKY!

MOM BROUGHT YA SOME MORE **BLANKETS** 'N STUFF!

WOW! THANKS! I DON'T KNOW **HOW** I WOULD'VE MADE IT THROUGH TH' WINTER WITHOUT YOU, MIZ 'POSSUM!

DON'T YOU **WORRY** ABOUT IT! AS LONG AS YOU'RE STUCK HERE IN OUR VALLEY, **I'LL** TAKE CARE OF YOU! **HERE!** I PACKED A PIE IN CASE YOU'RE HUNGRY!

DID YOU EVER FIND THOSE COUSINS OF YOURS?

NO, NOT YET. HAVE YOU SEEN **TED** SINCE I TALKED TO YOU LAST?

NOPE. DON'T KNOW MUCH ABOUT WHAT BUGS **DO** IN TH' WINTER, BUT I HAVEN'T SEEN WING **NOR** ANTENNEA OF TED SINCE TH' **SNOW** HIT....

SAY.... WASN'T THERE SOMEONE **ELSE** YOU WANTED ME TO FIND OUT ABOUT?

TED WAS GONNA TAKE ME TO SEE SOMEONE NAMED **THORN.**

OH, THAT'S RIGHT! NOPE, HAVEN'T FOUND OUT A **THING!** YOU SURE YOU HAVE ENOUGH BLANKETS?

YES, M'AM. SIGH. WELL, THANKS ANYWAY, MIZ 'POSSUM! IF THERE'S EVER ANYTHING I CAN DO--

AS A MATTER OF **FACT**, I'M ON MY WAY OVER TO MIZ HEDGEHOG'S PLACE, 'N' I WAS WONDERIN' IF YOU'D MIND WATCHIN' TH' KIDS?

ALL **RIGHT**! WE'RE GONNA STAY WITH FONE BONE!

ME?! BUT.... **I** DON'T KNOW ANYTHING ABOUT BABY 'POSSUMS!

IT'LL JUST BE FOR AN HOUR OR TWO! YOU BOYS BE **GOOD** NOW!

DON'T WORRY ABOUT **US**, MOM!

WELL,... C'MON, GUYS. YOU CAN HELP ME PUT THE **FINISHING** TOUCH ON MY HOUSE!

RUN INSIDE WHERE IT'S WARM.... I'LL JUST BE A SECOND!

WHOOP!

YIPPEE!

THERE WE GO! COZY AS AN IGLOO! BY THE TIME THIS MELTS, IT'LL BE **SPRING**, AN' THEN I'M **OUTTA** HERE!

SMASH! CRASH!

HEY, GUYS! TAKE IT **EASY** IN TH---

CRUNCH

34

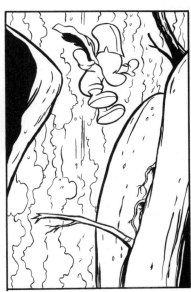

THOSE RAT CREATURES WOULD HAVE TO BE PRETTY STUPID TO FOLLOW ME ON TO THIS FRAIL, LITTLE BRANCH!

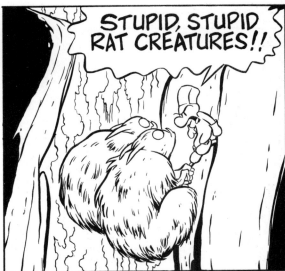

STUPID, STUPID RAT CREATURES!!

42

BONE! THERE YOU ARE! WE CAME AS FAST AS WE COULD! ARE YOU ALL RIGHT?

YAY!

HE'S SAFE!

I'M OKAY.... I HAD A LITTLE RUN-IN WITH A DRAGON, BUT THE IMPORTANT THING IS THAT WE'RE ALL SAFE!

A DRAGON? REALLY?

GET OUTTA TOWN!

SEE HOW HE IS WITH TH' KIDS? HE'S ALWAYS GOT A STORY!

IT'S NOT ENOUGH THAT HE CHASED OFF THOSE BULLIES... NOW HE'S TURNED IT INTO A YARN WITH A DRAGON IN IT!

ISN'T THAT PRECIOUS?

WHAT WAS THAT?

OH! I'M SORRY, BONE! TEE HEE! GO AHEAD AN' TELL TH' BOYS ABOUT TH' FEROCIOUS FIRE BREATHING DRAGON!

YEAH! TELL US! WERE YOU SCARED?

OF COURSE I WAS!

HE'S SO MODEST!

AND BRAVE!

WHAT HAPPENED, FONE BONE? DID YOU KILL TH' DRAGON?

WHAT HAPPENED TO YOUR HAT? DID THE DRAGON DO IT?

HE'S PULLIN' OUR TAILS! EVERYBODY KNOWS DRAGONS ARE MAKE BELIEVE!

AREN'T THEY?!

THAT'S ENOUGH QUESTIONS FOR NOW. UNCLE BONE MUST BE VERY TIRED. LET'S ALL GO HOME WHERE IT'S WARM AND SAFE, AND THEN BONE CAN TELL US ALL ABOUT HIS ADVENTURE!

MAYBE HE'D LIKE TO STOP AND CLEAN UP FIRST.

OH, YES! BY ALL **MEANS**! THERE'S A NICE, HOT **SPRING** JUST BACK OVER TH' HILL! WHY DON'T YOU STOP THERE TO FRESHEN UP! C'MON ALONG, BOYS! SAY THANK YOU TO UNCLE BONE!

THANK YOU!

DID HE REALLY SEE A DRAGON?

NOW DEAR...

HMMF! DID **TOO** SEE A DRAGON!

WHAT DO THEY **THINK**? I LIT MY **HEAD** ON FIRE TO KEEP WARM?

...AN' HOW COME THAT DRAGON KNEW I WAS BABYSITTING TH' **POSSUM** KIDS? WHAT'S HE DOIN'? **FOLLOWIN'** ME AROUND?

THIS PLACE IS **TOO** WIERD! THE FIRST SIGN OF SPRING I SEE.... POW! I'M TAKIN' OFF **RIGHT** THROUGH THOSE MOUNTAINS! WITH OR **WITHOUT** MY COUSINS!

SNAP!

UH, OH, WHAT WAS THAT?

♪ MMMMMM ♪

FOOM!

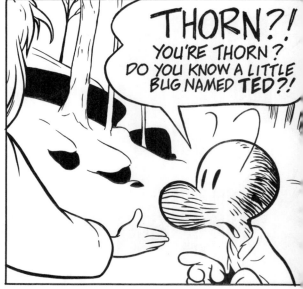

48

WHY, YES! I KNOW TED! HE'S A **VERY** GOOD FRIEND OF MINE!

HOTCHA! THIS IS **GREAT!**

I'VE BEEN LOOKIN' FOR YOU **ALL WINTER!!**

YOU HAVE? WHY?

TED! HE TOLD ME TO FIND YOU! HE SAID THAT YOU KNOW **EVERYTHING!**

WELL, THAT CERTAINLY **SOUNDS** LIKE TED.

GREAT! THEN YOU CAN HELP ME AND MY COUSINS GET BACK TO **BONEVILLE?**

COUSIN'S? YOU MEAN THERE'S **MORE** OF YOU?

YEAH! THEY'RE STUCK IN THIS VALLEY, TOO! BUT I HAVEN'T SEEN EITHER ONE OF 'EM SINCE WE GOT HIT BY THAT SWARM OF **LOCUSTS!**

YOU DON'T SAY.

Y'KNOW.... I **SHOULD'VE** ASKED THAT **DRAGON** IF HE'D SEEN MY COUSINS!

YOU SHOULD'VE ASKED **WHO**?

THE **DRAGON**! OH...WAIT A MINUTE! I GET IT! YOU DON'T BELIEVE IN DRAGONS **DO YOU**?

NO. SHOULD I?

NEVERMIND! I DON'T **CARE**!

ONCE I'M BACK IN **BONEVILLE**, I'LL NEVER EVEN HAVE TO **THINK** ABOUT DRAGONS OR THIS CRAZY VALLEY **AGAIN**!

WELL, I'D **LIKE** TO HELP....

WELL, C'MON! THERE'S NO TIME TO LOSE!!

...BUT... I'VE NEVER **HEARD** OF BONEVILLE.

THERE **IS** A LITTLE VILLAGE DOWN THE ROAD CALLED BARRELHAVEN... DOES THAT HELP?

...WHAT'S WRONG?

NOTHIN'

FONE BONE?

OH.... I DON'T BELONG IN THIS FOREST. MY HOME'S ON THE OTHER SIDE OF THE MOUNTAINS...

I'M SURE WE CAN GET YOU THROUGH THE MOUNTAINS AS SOON AS THE SNOW MELTS!

IT'S NOT JUST THAT! EVEN IF I **COULD** GET THROUGH THE MOUNTAINS, I'D **NEVER** FIND MY WAY BACK ACROSS THE DESERT. YOU WERE MY LAST HOPE.

WELL, LET'S JUST CONCENTRATE ON FINDING YOUR COUSINS. YOU'RE **SURE** THEY'RE HERE IN THE VALLEY?

PRETTY SURE, UNLESS THE RAT CREATURES GOT 'EM.

DID YOU SAY **RAT CREATURES**?

LET ME GUESS.... YOU DON'T **BELIEVE** IN RAT CREATURES.

OH, YES I **DO**! HAVE YOU SEEN ONE **RECENTLY**?

I SAW **TWO** OF 'EM! TH' DRAGON CHASED 'EM OFF!

NOW LISTEN TO ME....THIS IS IMPORTANT! YOU'RE NOT FOOLING AROUND? YOU **REALLY** SAW TWO RAT CREATURES?

YEAH! I REALLY SAW A **DRAGON**, TOO! LOOK AT MY **HEAD**! WHAT DO YOU THINK **THIS** IS? A **TAN**?!

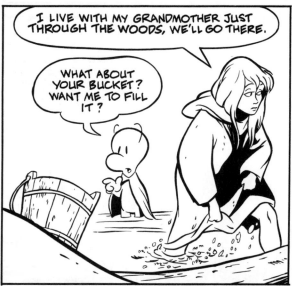

Next: Phoney Bone

MY! YOU MUST'VE **ENJOYED** YOUR FIRST NIGHT IN A HOUSE AFTER SLEEPING IN THE **WOODS**! YOU DIDN'T EVEN **HEAR** ME WHEN I CAME DOWNSTAIRS!

CAKES?

HERE'S YOUR CAKES! AND HERE'S SOME TEA!

THENK YOU.

HELLO? ARE YOU **AWAKE** YET, FONE BONE? IT'S **ME, THORN!**

THORN?

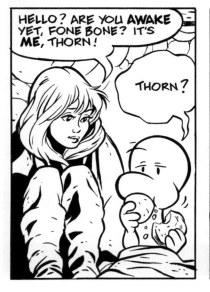

AH! **YOU'RE** AWAKE! GOOD! NOW EAT YOUR BREAKFAST! WE'VE GOT A LOT TO **DO** TODAY! GRAN'MA BEN IS COMING HOME FROM THE VILLAGE, AND I WANT TO CLEAN THE PLACE UP BEFORE SHE GETS HERE!

SHE'S COMING HOME **TODAY**?

THAT'S **RIGHT**! SHE GOES INTO **BARRELHAVEN** EVERY SPRING TO SHOW OFF HER BEST **RACING** COWS!

YOUR **GRAN'MA** RACES COWS?!

YEAH! SHE'S PRETTY **GOOD**, TOO! THERE'S HARDLY A COW IN THE WHOLE **VALLEY** THAT CAN BEAT HER IN A **100 YARD DASH**!

HUH! I'M **DEFINITELY** LOOKING FORWARD TO **MEETING** THIS LADY!

OH, IT'S A **BIG EVENT** HERE IN THE SPRING! PEOPLE BET **CHICKENS** AND **GOATS** -- SOME FOLKS BET THEIR WHOLE **LIVESTOCK** ON HER!
> IF YOU WANT TO MAKE A GOOD IMPRESSION, BE SURE TO COMPLIMENT HER ON HER **COWS**! SHE'S **REAL** PROUD OF HER COWS!

I'LL TRY TO REMEMBER THAT.

NOW, IF YOU'RE DONE EATING, WHY DON'T WE GO GET SOME WATER?

OKAY BY ME! LET'S **DO IT**!

IF YOU FINISH UP THE DISHES, I'LL GO SPLIT SOME FIREWOOD.

!

NOW **WAIT** A MINUTE, THORN!

WHAT?

WHERE **I** COME FROM, WHAT **YOU** JUST SAID IS **BACKWARDS!**

CHOPPIN' FIREWOOD IS A **MANLY** THING! AN' SINCE **I'M** THE MAN, I'LL DO THE **MANLY** THING!

WHAT 'MANLY' KIND OF THING DO YOU CALL THAT?

CHIN-UPS! GO DO TH' DISHES!

HOW ABOUT IF WE GET THE FIREWOOD **LATER**?

SIGH.

SO... DO YOU THINK YOUR GRAN'MA WILL MIND ME **STAYIN'** WITH YOU GUYS? I MEAN-- I DON'T WANNA CAUSE ANY PROBLEMS!

SHE WON'T MIND! SHE WOULDN'T MAKE YOU GO BACK OUT IN THE **WOODS**-- ESPECIALLY WITH THOSE **RAT CREATURES** AROUND!

I HOPE NOT.

JUST DO ME ONE FAVOR! WHEN GRAN'MA BEN GETS HERE, **TRY** NOT TO MENTION YOUR FRIEND THE **DRAGON**!

WHY NOT?

BECAUSE DRAGONS DON'T **EXIST**, THAT'S WHY!

WHAT DO YOU **MEAN**? YOU BELIEVE IN **RAT CREATURES**! WHY DON'T YOU BELIEVE IN **DRAGONS**?

BECAUSE **EVERYBODY** BELIEVES IN RAT CREATURES! BUT **YOU'RE** THE ONLY ONE WHO'S EVER SEEN A **DRAGON**!

I DON'T BELIEVE IT!

DO YOU HAVE DRAGONS BACK IN BONEVILLE?

OF COURSE NOT!

WELL?

WELL, WE DON'T HAVE BIG MOUTHED, DROOLING, RAT-LIKE MONSTERS, EITHER! UNLESS YOU COUNT MY COUSIN PHONEY BONE!

AN' YOU KNOW WHAT ELSE? I THINK THAT DRAGON IS FOLLOWIN' ME AROUND!

FONE BONE! WE'VE BEEN OVER THIS A HUNDRED TIMES!

BUT I'M TELLIN' YA, I SAW ONE! HE HAD A GOATEE, 'N' A CIGARET, 'N' BIG OL' HAIRY EARS LIKE THIS!

DRAGONS ARE MAKE BELIEVE! YOU WERE SEEING THINGS!

THANKS FOR THE SUPPORT, THORN! YOU KNOW, THAT'S WHAT THE DRAGON WANTS YOU TO THINK! HE DOESN'T WANT YOU TO KNOW HE EXISTS!

ACTUALLY, I JUST WANT HER TO THINK YOU'RE NUTS!

OH, SHUT UP!

YOU **HAVEN'T**? YOU MUST'VE HAD A DEPRIVED CHILDHOOD. **THESE** I BROUGHT FOR PHONEY BONE... THEY'RE **FINANCIAL MAGAZINES**!

DIDN'T YOU BRING ANYTHING FOR YOURSELF?

SURE! THIS IS **MOBY DICK!** IT'S MY **FAVORITE** BOOK. I'VE READ IT **THREE TIMES!**

WHAT'S IT ABOUT?

UH... ARE YOU **SURE** YOU WANT TO KNOW? EVERY TIME I TRY TO TELL PEOPLE ABOUT MOBY DICK THEIR **EYES** GLAZE OVER!

TRY ME.

OKAY! IT'S ABOUT A WHALING VOYAGE, AN' THIS GUY **ISHMAEL**-----❊

Z

HA. HA. **VERY** FUNNY.

WHAT ELSE HAVE YOU GOT IN HERE?

LET'S SEE... A BLANKET.... AN OLD MAP THAT SMILEY FOUND......

THAT'S ABOUT **IT!** THE ONE THING I **DIDN'T** BRING ENOUGH OF WAS **FOOD** AND **WATER!** WELL, TH'**TWO** THINGS........

WHY ARE YOU MAKING THAT FACE?

I DON'T KNOW.... SOMETHING ABOUT THIS MAP IS FAMILIAR...

REALLY? SMILEY FOUND IT OUT IN TH' DESERT RIGHT BEFORE WE GOT SPLIT UP.

IT REMINDS ME OF A DREAM I USED TO HAVE...

WHOA. AND YOU THINK **MY** STORIES ARE STRANGE!

ARE YOU OKAY?

I'M FINE. LET'S JUST FORGET IT. C'MON. GRAN'MA WILL BE HERE SOON....

64

SLURK
GUKK
BURRRP!

SIGH.

WHAT A **TRAVESTY**! TH' MOST CHERISHED AND **RESPECTED** (NOT TO MENTION WEALTHIEST!) BONE IN BONEVILLE -- OUT IN TH' **WOODS** -- FENDING OFF TH' ELEMENTS WITH HIS BARE HANDS!

FORCED TO **EKE** OUT A MISERABLE EXISTANCE **AMIDST TH' ROCKS 'N' MUD!!**

OH, CRUEL, CRUEL, FATE! WHY HAVE YOU ABANDONED YOUR MOST BELOVED SON?!

GOD, I PITY ME.

HEY, YOU! WAKE UP!

MM?

68

DO YOU LIKE APPLE PIE, FONE BONE?

LIKE IT? IT'S MY FAVORITE **HOBBY!**

WELL, DON'T GET **TOO** EXCITED!

THIS IS FOR **GRAN'MA**-- SHE **LOVES** MY SPECIAL APPLE PIE....

..... AND WE WANT TO BE **REAL** NICE TO GRAN'MA BEFORE WE ASK ABOUT YOU **STAYING HERE!**

CLINK CLINK

71

WHAT HAPPENED TO **PHONEY**?

-- UH, OH --

I **THINK** HE'S IN THE **FIREPLACE!**

I'M **COMIN'**, PHONEY'!

HURRY, GRAN'MA! HE'S **STUCK** IN THE **FIREPLACE!**

OH, MY **GOODNESS!** HE'LL RUIN TH' DINNER!

HANG ON! I'LL GET YOU OUT!

FONE BONE! SAVE ME! THAT **CRAZY** OLD LADY TRIED TO **KILL ME!!**

WELL, BLESS MY **BUTTONS!** WHAT HAVE WE GOT HERE?

WATCH OUT! DON'T LET HER GET A HOLD OF YOU!

H-- H'LO, MA'M!

DO **YOU** LIKE COWS? I KNOW YOUR **FRIEND** DOESN'T.

I DON'T LIKE TO **RIDE** 'EM, YOU OL' **BAT!**

FONE BONE LOVES COWS!

SORRY, DEAR. YOU CAN'T KEEP HIM.

BUT--

NO BUTS. I DON'T WANT ANY PETS RUNNING AROUND TH' HOUSE.

GRAN'MA! THEY'RE NOT PETS!

CAN YOU MILK 'EM? IF YOU CAN'T MILK 'EM, THEY'RE PETS!

THAT'S IT! I'M OUTTA HERE!

GRAN'MA!

SAY.... IS THAT APPLE PIE I SMELL?

YES! I BAKED ONE OF MY SPECIAL PIES JUST FOR YOU!

WHAT A SWEET THING YOU ARE!

QUICK! WHILE SHE'S DISTRACTED!

HOLD IT! THORN THINKS GRAN'MA BEN CAN HELP US GET BACK TO BONEVILLE!

IT'S NOT WORTH IT! LET GO OF ME!

WOULD YOU WAIT A MINUTE?!! WE CAN EXPLAIN EVERYTHING!

HELP! HELP! THEY'VE DESTROYED MY COUSIN'S BRAIN!! OH, MY GOD! THEY'VE ALREADY MILKED YOU, HAVEN'T THEY?!!

GRAN'MA, THEY'RE BONES! THEY COME FROM A PLACE CALLED BONEVILLE! AND THEY NEED OUR HELP TO GET BACK!

WHERE'S SMILEY?

SMILEY? I THOUGHT HE WAS WITH YOU!

YOU HAVEN'T SEEN HIM SINCE WE SPLIT UP? BUT I KNOW HE'S IN TH' VALLEY! I FOUND ONE OF HIS CIGAR BUTTS!

TH' LAST TIME I SAW THAT CHOWDER HEAD, HE WAS SAYIN' HOW COOL IT WAS THAT WE WERE ABOUT TO BE PULVERIZED BY LOCUSTS!

YEAH! THAT'S TH' LAST TIME I SAW HIM, TOO...

AW, QUIT YER WORRYIN'! WHY DON'T YA INTRODUCE ME TO YER GOOD LOOKIN' FRIEND, HERE?

OH! UH... PHONEY, THIS IS THORN! THORN, PHONEY.

SO, WHAT'VE YOU BEEN DOIN' WITH MY COUSIN? YOU TWO GOT A LITTLE THING GOIN', OR WHAT?

PHONEY!

NO, HUH? FIGURES! WHAT'D YA DO? BORE HER TO DEATH TALKIN' ABOUT MOBY DICK?

74

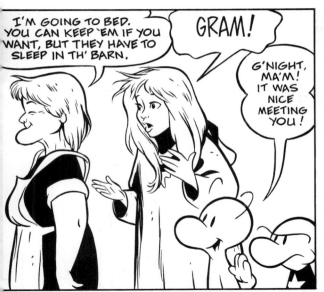

I'M GOING TO BED. YOU CAN KEEP 'EM IF YOU WANT, BUT THEY HAVE TO SLEEP IN TH' BARN.

GRAM!

G'NIGHT, MA'M! IT WAS NICE MEETING YOU!

FONE BONE, COULD I TALK TO YOU FOR A MOMENT? OUTSIDE?

YES.

WELL, GO AHEAD! I AIN'T STOPPIN' YA!

THIS ISN'T GOING QUITE THE WAY WE **PLANNED**, IS IT? TELL ME... IS HE **ALWAYS** LIKE THIS?

PRETTY MUCH.

HMM. GRAN'MA'S GOING BACK TO **BARRELHAVEN** IN A FEW DAYS FOR THE SPRING FESTIVAL. IF WE CAN JUST KEEP THOSE TWO **CALM** UNTIL **THEN**, WE CAN ALL GO INTO TOWN TOGETHER TO LOOK FOR YOUR OTHER COUSIN.

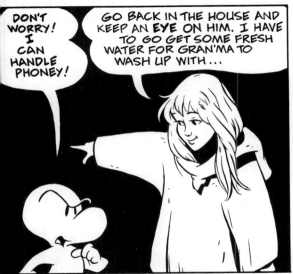

DON'T WORRY! I CAN HANDLE PHONEY!

GO BACK IN THE HOUSE AND KEEP AN **EYE** ON HIM. I HAVE TO GO GET SOME FRESH WATER FOR GRAN'MA TO WASH UP WITH...

OKAY, PHONEY! WE HAVE TO GET A COUPLE OF THINGS **STRAIGHT---**

Next: Barrelhaven

GOOD! I'VE GOTTA GO FIND **THORN**... I PROMISED I'D HELP HER CHURN BUTTER TODAY!

YEAH, YEAH. STICK SOME HAY IN MY TEETH AN' CALL ME GOOBER!

CHEER UP, PHONEY! **BREAKFAST** WILL BE READY SOON!

RRRRR.

MORNIN', BONE!

GOOD MORNIN', GRAN'MA! YOU ALL SET FOR OUR BIG TRIP INTO **BARRELHAVEN** TOMORROW?

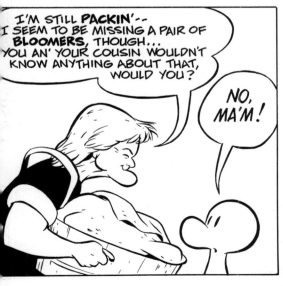

I'M STILL **PACKIN'**-- I SEEM TO BE MISSING A PAIR OF **BLOOMERS**, THOUGH... YOU AN' YOUR COUSIN WOULDN'T KNOW ANYTHING ABOUT THAT, WOULD YOU?

NO, MA'M!

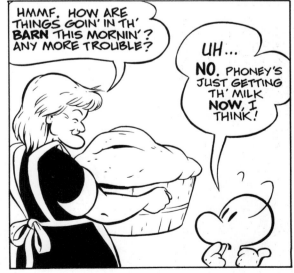

HMMF. HOW ARE THINGS GOIN' IN TH' **BARN** THIS MORNIN'? ANY MORE TROUBLE?

UH... **NO.** PHONEY'S JUST GETTING TH' MILK **NOW**, I THINK!

PHONEY! DID YOU DO SOMETHING WITH GRAN'MA BEN'S **BLOOMERS**?

YEH, I TOOK 'EM OFF TH' CLOTHESLINE AND NAILED 'EM UP ON TH' SIDE OF TH' BARN.

YOU DID WHAT?!!

I KINDA MADE A LITTLE HOLE IN TH' WALL, AND THOSE WERE THE BIGGEST THINGS I COULD FIND TO COVER IT UP!

YOU'RE REALLY **PUSHIN'** IT, **THIS** TIME, PHONEY!

YOU CAN'T TALK THAT WAY TO ME! I'M YOUR **COUSIN**! I'M TH' **RICHEST BONE** IN **BONEVILLE**!

YOU **WERE** TH' RICHEST BONE IN BONEVILLE! AN' IT WAS YOUR **MONEY GRUBBIN' SCHEMES** THAT GOT US **INTO** THIS MESS, REMEMBER?

DO YOU **HAVE** TO KEEP BRINGING THAT UP?! SO I GOT US RUN OUT OF BONEVILLE, AND A **LYNCH MOB** CHASED US FOR TWO WEEKS! **JEEZ**! ONE LITTLE MISTAKE, AND I GOTTA **HEAR** ABOUT IT TH' REST OF MY **LIFE**?!

MAYBE YOU'LL THINK **TWICE** NEXT TIME BEFORE YOU BUILD AN **ORPHANAGE** ON A **HAZARDOUS WASTE LANDFILL**!!

WHAT IS **WRONG** WITH **THAT**?! THAT'S **TWO** COMMUNITY SERVICES ROLLED INTO **ONE**!! IT WAS TH' **ULTIMATE TAX SHELTER**!

YOU **NEVER** LEARN, DO YOU?

I **SHOULDA** STUCK WITH MY **FIRST** IDEA!

WHAT? COMBINING A **SLAUGHTER HOUSE** WITH A **PETTING ZOO**?! OH, YEAH! **THAT** WAS BRILLIANT!

AHH! WHAT DO **YOU** KNOW?

CAN'T YOU MAKE IT THROUGH **ONE MORE DAY** WITHOUT GETTING US IN **TROUBLE**? WE'RE GOIN' INTO TOWN WITH GRAN'MA **TOMORROW**!

WHAT ARE WE WAITIN' FOR **HER** FOR? LET'S BLOW THIS POPSICLE STAND **NOW**!

TOMORROW IS TH' FIRST DAY OF TH' **SPRING FAIR**! THIS'LL BE OUR **BEST SHOT** AT FINDING SMILEY BONE!

GRAN'MA SAID THAT **LAST** WEEK PEOPLE WERE ALREADY COMIN' IN FROM **ALL OVER** TH' VALLEY----SETTIN' UP **BOOTHS** AN' GETTIN' READY!

WELL, **I** FIGURE-- IF SMILEY'S SOMEWHERE IN TH' VALLEY, HE'S **BOUND** TO HAVE HEARD ABOUT GRAN'MA'S **COW RACE**! YOU **KNOW** HOW MUCH HE LIKES TO BET ON **RACES**!

HO-- BACK UP! YOU MEAN PEOPLE ACTUALLY BET **MONEY** ON THAT OL' BAG TO BEAT A **COW** IN A **FOOT RACE**?

I **KNOW!** IT'S **CRAZY**, BUT THORN SAYS IT'S A BIG **DEAL** HERE! SOME FOLKS BET EVERYTHING THEY'VE **GOT**!

OKAY, FONE BONE! **I'LL** BE GOOD! I POSITIVELY **GUARANTEE** YOU WON'T HEAR ANOTHER **PEEP** OUTTA ME ALL DAY!

REALLY?

YEAH, NOW GET OFF MY BACK! GO CHURN SOME BUTTER WITH THORN! I'VE GOT STUFF TO DO!

WHAT? WHAT ARE YOU UP TO?

NOTHING! I SAID I WON'T MESS UP YOUR PLAN TO GO INTO TOWN TO LOOK FOR SMILEY, AN' I **MEANT** IT!

AND I WON'T HEAR A **PEEP** OUTTA YOU TH' REST OF TH' **DAY**, RIGHT?

RIGHT! JEEZ! DO YA WANT IT IN **WRITING**?!

DO YOU HAVE A PIECE OF PAPER?

I THINK I HEAR THORN CALLIN' YA.

REALLY?! OKAY, PHONEY! SEE YA TONIGHT!

YEP. YOU WON'T HEAR A **PEEP** OUTTA **ME**, 'CAUSE **I** AIN'T GONNA BE HERE!

FONE BONE WON'T MIND IF I BORROW A FEW OF HIS THINGS.... I MIGHT NEED 'EM ON MY WAY TO TOWN....

SOUNDS LIKE A LOTTA **MONEY'S** GONNA CHANGE HANDS TOMORROW, AN' I DON'T SEE WHY GRAN'MA BEN SHOULD **HOG** IT ALL!

NO, SIRREE! IF THERE'S **BOOKMAKIN'** TO BE DONE, **I'M** TH' MAN TO **DO** IT!

84

HEY, THORN! WHERE WE GOIN'?

DOWN TO THE SPRINGS!

OH, FONE BONE, YOU'RE GOING TO **LOVE** THE FESTIVAL! WE'LL SEE JUGGLERS, AND TUMBLERS, AND SINGERS! AND MY **FAVORITE** PART--THE **BOOTHS!**

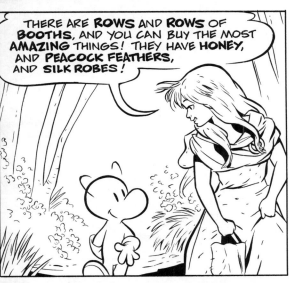

THERE ARE **ROWS** AND **ROWS** OF **BOOTHS**, AND YOU CAN BUY THE MOST **AMAZING** THINGS! THEY HAVE **HONEY**, AND **PEACOCK FEATHERS**, AND **SILK ROBES!**

I USUALLY ONLY GET TO LOOK-- BUT **THIS** YEAR I'M GOING TO GET A BOTTLE OF **DYE** FROM THE SOUTH, AND I'M GOING TO MAKE A BEAUTIFUL **BLUE DRESS!**

HOW COME WE DIDN'T BRING ANY BUCKETS TO TO CARRY TH' WATER BACK IN?

WE'RE NOT GETTING WATER.

WE'RE TAKING A BATH!

A BATH? WHAT **KIND** OF BATH?

OHMYGOSH

YOU WANT TO GET CLEANED UP FOR THE FESTIVAL, DON'T YOU? C'MON!

86

I'M HIS COUSIN.

HIS **COUSIN**? ALL **RIGHT**! YOU WANNA PLAY WITH US?

WE'RE LEARNIN' HOW TO HANG BY OUR TAILS!

NO, THANKS. I'M ON MY WAY INTO TOWN.

HEY, MISTER! YOU KNOW TH' **WAY** INTO TOWN?

YEAH. WHY?

IT'S **THAT** WAY.

OH! RIGHT!

THANKS, KID! WHEN I COME BACK, I'LL BRING YOU A **CARROT**!

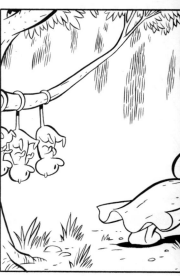

A CARROT? WHAT'S HE THINK WE ARE? RABBITS?

WHAT A DORK.

LUCKY THING I RAN INTO THOSE KIDS! AS SOON AS I'M BACK ON TH' RIGHT PATH, I SHOULD GET TO BARRELHAVEN IN **NO TIME**!

TH' FIRST THING I GOTTA DO, IS HIT TH' LOCAL TAVERN, AN' FIND OUT WHO'S IN TOWN TO BET ON TH' RACE...

SNIFF

SNIFF! SNIFF! *OOOH!* MAN! SOMETHING AROUND HERE SURE **STINKS!**

JEEZ! IT'S GETTIN' **WORSE!**

WHOA.

WHAT TH' **HECK** ARE **THOSE** THINGS?

UH, OH! SOMEBODY'S COMIN'!

GET UP YOU TWO.

ZZRT SNORT!

WHA--?

GET UP BEFORE I CRUSH YOUR HEADS.

KINGDOK!

KINGDOK?

SIRE! WHAT ARE **YOU** DOING HERE? MAY I KISS YOUR FEET? I WISH I HAD SOME **QUICHE** I COULD OFFER YOU--

W-WOULD YOU LIKE SOME OF THE SMALL DEAD THING I FOUND UNDER A BUSH? I WAS SAVING HALF FOR LATER, BUT YOU'RE MORE THAN WELCOME--

QUIET! I'VE HAD SCOUTS OUT LOOKING FOR YOU TWO!

Y-YOU HAVE? HOW FLATTERING! I'M FLATTERED! ARE YOU FLATTERED?

YOU TWO ARE STARTING TO MAKE ME LOOK BAD. THE **HOODED ONE** HAS SUMMONED YOU BOTH TO A HIGH COUNCIL-- **TONIGHT!**

THE HOODED ONE--

HAS SOMETHING HAPPENED?

EVERYTHING'S READY FOR TOMORROW. I JUST WISH I COULD SHAKE THIS **GITCHY FEELIN'** I GOT!

DID YOU FIND TH' LITTLE SQUIRT?

NO. AN' MY **BOOTS** AN' **KNAPSACK** ARE MISSING TOO! I THINK HE WENT INTO TOWN WITHOUT US!

WE LOOKED FOR HIM, BUT THERE'S NO SIGN OF HIM ON THE ROAD. WE WENT ALL THE WAY TO OLD MAN'S CAVE BEFORE IT GOT TOO DARK. I'M SURE WE'LL FIND HIM AT THE FAIR TOMORROW.

HMM. I DON'T LIKE IT. AN' THERE'S A BAD MOON OUT TONIGHT, TOO.

RUN BACK TO TH' BARN, AN' GET YOUR BLANKET. I THINK YOU BETTER COME IN TH' HOUSE WITH US TONIGHT.

OKAY

94

WE TRIED TO SPY.... BUT THE DRAGON TREDS A WIDE CIRCLE AROUND HIM...

THE CREATURE IS ON A SMALL FARM NEAR THE HOT SPRINGS... HE STAYS WITH THE OLD COW WOMAN ...MOTHER BEN.....

.... THESE ARE GRAVE TIDINGS....IT WOULD NOT BE WELL FOR THE DRAGON TO LEARN OF OUR PLANS....

....IF WE MUST RISK A CONFRONTATION..... WE MUST DO IT NOW,... WHILE THE DRAGON'S SUSPICIONS SLEEP....

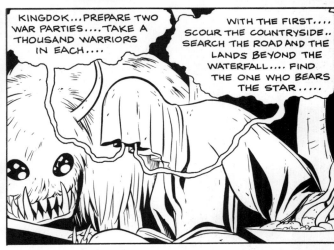

KINGDOK...PREPARE TWO WAR PARTIES....TAKE A THOUSAND WARRIORS IN EACH....

WITH THE FIRST.... SCOUR THE COUNTRYSIDE.. SEARCH THE ROAD AND THE LANDS BEYOND THE WATERFALL.... FIND THE ONE WHO BEARS THE STAR.....

....IF THE DRAGON IS STILL WATCHING....THIS ACTIVITY WILL DRAW HIM OFF...LEAVING THE OLD COW WOMAN UNGUARDED.....

SEND THE SECOND PARTY TO THE FARM HOUSE..... ...DESTROY IT....... ...KILL THE NEW CREATURE...

LET US HOPE THAT THE DEATH OF THIS FONE BONE WILL CAUSE THE DRAGON TO LEAVE THE VALLEY AND RETURN TO DEREN GARD....

...GO NOW.... WE ATTACK TONIGHT

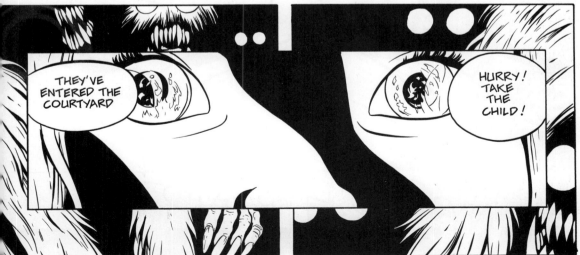

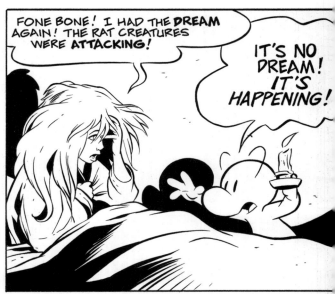

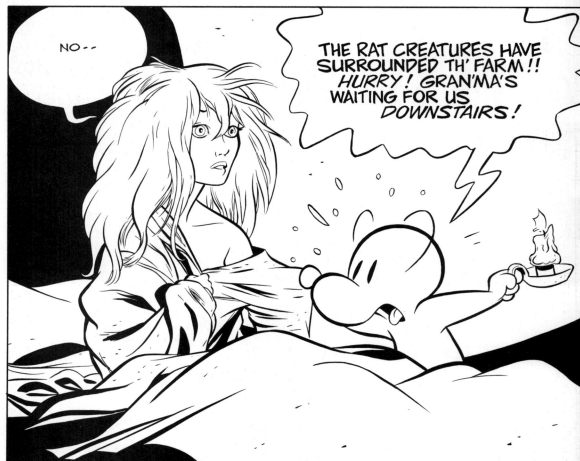

Next: TRAPPED

CRASSS SPLINTER!

KKKRRRKKK-V-V

OKAY, KIDS! RUN!

CRUNCH

UH...

NOW, BONE!

WE CAN'T JUST LEAVE YOU HERE!

COME ON, FONE BONE!

DON'T WORRY ABOUT ME--

BIF!

SPLAT!

I FOUGHT TH' RATS BACK IN TH' BIG WAR!

OHMYGOSH

THUD THUD! WAK!

101

OHMYGOSH

OHMYGOSH

GET UP! GET UP!

WHAT HAPPENED?

WHY ARE WE STOPPING?

Shh! WE HAVE TO GO BACK! GRAN'MA NEEDS OUR **HELP**!

NOW YOU'RE WORRIED ABOUT GRAN'MA?!

THERE'S TOO **MANY**! SHE DIDN'T KNOW THE WOODS WERE **FULL** OF MONSTERS!

AAAAH!

105

CREEEAK

IT **IS** YOU! THANK **GOODNESS** I'VE **FOUND** YOU!!

YA **MEAN** IT, PHONEY? YOU'RE **HAPPY** TO SEE ME?

DARN RIGHT!! FONE BONE WOULDN'T LET ME **LEAVE** THIS STUPID VALLEY UNLESS I **FOUND** YOU FIRST!

AW, SHUCKS-- IT'S GOOD TO SEE YOU **TOO,** CUZ!

THIS CALLS FOR A **TOAST!** LET ME BUY YOU A **DRINK,** OL' **BUDDY!**

OKAY BY **ME,** OL' **PAL!**

HERE'S TO GOIN' **HOME!**

TO BONEVILLE!

CLINK

TO BONEVILLE!

GLUG! GLUG!

AHH!

SMEK

SMEK

WHADDYA SAY WE HAVE ANOTHER ROUND ON **YOU,** OL' FRIEND!

SURE! WHY NOT? I GOT A FEELIN' MY **LUCK'S** ABOUT TO **CHANGE!** -- **GUESS** WHERE FONE BONE IS **RIGHT NOW!** HE'S WITH **GRAN'MA BEN!** YOU KNOW-- TH' OLD LADY THAT RACES **COWS!**

AH! YOU'RE IN TOWN FOR TH' **COW RACE!** ME TOO! THERE'S GONNA BE SOME HEAVY **BETTIN'** GOIN' ON!

SO I'VE HEARD!

IS ANYBODY DOIN' TH' **BOOKMAKIN'**?

NOT YET....BUT FROM WHAT I'VE PICKED UP--- YOUR FRIEND **GRAN'MA** IS TH' **ODDS ON** FAVORITE!

GREAT! PERFECT! HOW MUCH TIME DO WE HAVE?

ONE WEEK.

EXCELLENT! I GOT AN **IDEA** THAT'LL MAKE US A **LOTTA** MONEY!

UH, OH! I HOPE THIS ISN'T GONNA BE ONE OF THOSE **SILLY** IDEAS YOU USED TO PULL BACK IN **BONEVILLE!**

WHAT?! WHAT ARE YOU **TALKIN'** ABOUT? **WHAT** SILLY IDEAS?!

REMEMBER TH' **FIRST** TIME YOU GOT US RUN OUT OF TOWN? YOU OPENED UP A CHAIN OF FRANCHISES-- **BONE ENVIRONMENTAL**: NUCLEAR REACTOR AND ENDLESS SALAD BARS!

THAT WASN'T A **SILLY IDEA!** TH' **LETTUCE** WOULDN'T SPOIL FOR **DECADES!**

WHAT ABOUT TH' **SECOND** TIME YOU GOT US RUN OUT? WHEN YOU STARTED **THE NEW AGE SCHOOL OF LAMAZE AND BUNGY-JUMPING!** EVEN I KNEW **THAT** WAS DUMB!

OH, YEAH, YOU'RE A **BRILLIANT** JUDGE!

NOW-- WHERE ARE WE GONNA FIND YOU A **COW SUIT?**

WHAT? I GET TO WEAR A **COW SUIT?! COOL!** HAVE ANOTHER **BEER**, PARTNER!

112

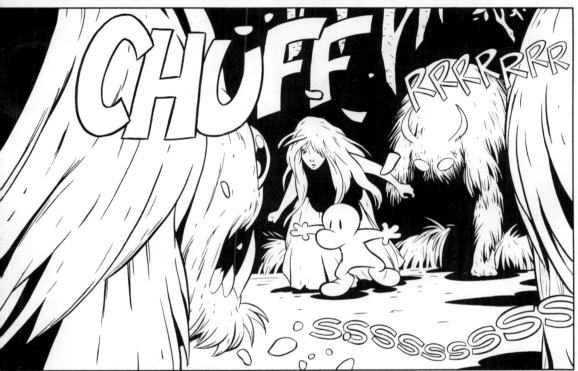

114

....DEFIANCE WILL NOT BE TOLORATED........ ....ONCE **WE** RETURN ORDER TO THE VALLEY......

STAY BACK!

SNIFF! SNIFF!

WAIT A MINUTE! WAIT A MINUTE!

DO YOU **SMELL** THAT?!

IT'S BRIMSTONE! IT'S THE **DRAGON**! HE'S **HERE**!

OH, NO.

RELAX, THORN! EVERYTHING'S GONNA BE **OKAY**!

FONE BONE! WHAT ARE YOU DOING?!

I KNOW **YOU** DON'T BELIEVE IN DRAGONS, BUT **THESE GUYS** DO! WATCH **THIS**!

HE DID IT! YES! I TOLD YOU THERE WAS A DRAGON! I TOLD YOU!

MR. DRAGON...

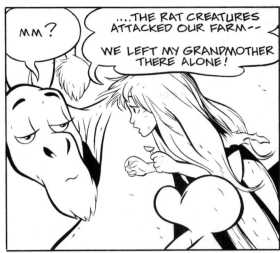

MM?

....THE RAT CREATURES ATTACKED OUR FARM-- WE LEFT MY GRANDMOTHER THERE ALONE!

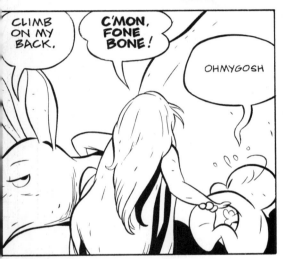

CLIMB ON MY BACK.

C'MON, FONE BONE!

OHMYGOSH

HOLD TIGHT!

HURRY!

Next: **PHONEY'S INFERNO**

121

BOWEL
I CAN'T BELIEVE IT!
THEY DESTROYED YOUR GRAN'MA'S HOUSE!
LET ME DOWN!!
WAIT A MINUTE--

...I KNOW IT LOOKS BAD, BUT WE NEED TO BE CAREFUL! WE'RE NOT GONNA HELP YOUR GRANDMOTHER BY RUSHIN' OUT IN TH' OPEN!
WE NEED TO MAKE SURE THERE'S NO RAT CREATURES HANGIN' AROUND...

CRUNCH! TINK!

THORN? IS THAT YOU, DEAR?

OH, GOOD! YOU'RE SAFE!

GRAN'MA--!

ARE YOU ALL RIGHT?

OF COURSE I AM, DEAR! *I* FOUGHT TH' RATS BACK IN TH' **BIG** WAR! BESIDES, I WASN'T **REALLY** IN DANGER...

...WHEN YOU AN' **BONE** LEFT TH' HOUSE, ALL TH' **FIGHT** WENT OUT OF 'EM! I WAS **MUCH** MORE WORRIED ABOUT **YOU!**

WE ALMOST GOT CAUGHT, BUT THE **DRAGON** SAVED US!

C'MON, TED.

GRAN'MA! WHAT ARE YOU DOING?! THE DRAGON JUST SAVED OUR LIVES!

NOT NOW, THORN. MR. BONE FROM BONEVILLE AN' I HAVE TO HAVE A LITTLE CHAT!

AND **YOU** HAVE A LOT OF THINGS TO DO BEFORE WE LEAVE FOR TH' **SPRING FAIR!**

THE **FAIR**?! YOU'RE NOT STILL WORRIED ABOUT YOUR **COW RACE**?!

WHAT ABOUT **PHONEY BONE** AN' **SMILEY**? WE HAVE TO **FIND** THEM!

BONE AND I WILL HITCH UP TH' CART. **YOU** BE A SWEETHEART AND PUT OUT TH' **FIRE** ON TH' **ROOF!**

SHE'S NOT EVEN **LISTENING** TO US! CAN YOU **BELIEVE** SHE WANTS TO GO TO TH' **FAIR**?!

ARE YOU **KIDDING**? I STILL CAN'T GET OVER TH' FACT THAT SHE HAS A **FIRST NAME!**

DEAR . . . I'M NOT A **COMPLETE** NINCOMPOOP! WE'LL BE **SAFER** IN TOWN! **AND**, WITH ANY LUCK, WE'LL BE ABLE TO FIND HIS **COUSINS!**

BUT --

PLEASE, THORN! WE **HAVE** TO **GO!** WE DON'T KNOW IF THEY'RE **SAFE!**

YOU'RE RIGHT! I'LL TAKE CARE OF THE ROOF!

WE PACKED EVERYTHING LAST NIGHT, SO TH' LUGGAGE IS ALREADY OUT IN TH' BARN. COME JOIN US WHEN YOU GET DONE.

C'MON, BONE!

GRAN'MA? WHAT **WAS** THAT WITH YOU AN' TH' **DRAGON**? DO YOU GUYS **KNOW** EACH OTHER?

I'LL ASK TH' QUESTIONS! I WANNA KNOW WHY THOSE MONSTERS WERE AFTER **YOU** . . . AN' I WANT TH' **TRUTH!**

I HAVE **NO** IDEA! **HONEST!** I'VE NEVER DONE **ANYTHING** TO THEM!

WHAT ABOUT THAT SHIFTY **COUSIN** OF YOURS? YOU THINK **PHONEY BONE** MIGHT'VE HAD SOME DEALIN'S WITH 'EM?

NO, MA'M! WE DON'T **HAVE** RAT CREATURES BACK WHERE WE COME FROM!

IN FACT, WE NEVER EVEN **HEARD** OF RAT CREATURES BEFORE WE GOT RUN OUT OF BONEVILLE!

WELL, ACTUALLY, **I** WASN'T RUN OUTTA BONEVILLE -- **PHONEY** WAS! SMILEY AN' I JUST HELPED HIM GET AWAY!

WHAT'D HE **DO**?

PHONEY DECIDED HE WAS GONNA RUN FOR **MAYOR!** HIS CAMPAIGN SLOGAN WAS: "AN' I'VE GOT TH' MONEY TO **DO** IT, **TOO!**"

SO TH' BONES RAN HIM OUTTA TOWN FOR **THAT**, HUH? WELL, **GOOD** FOR THEM!

NO. ANYBODY CAN RUN FOR MAYOR. EVEN **PHONEY!**

THAT GREEDY, LITTLE, **LOUDMOUTH?** NOT IN MY TOWN HE COULDN'T!

WELL, HE CAN IN BONEVILLE. ANYWAY, HE WANTED TO MAKE THE **OFFICIAL** ANNOUNCEMENT A BIG **SOCIAL EVENT**, SO HE DECIDED TO THROW A PICNIC DOWN ON TH' BANKS OF TH' ROLLING BONE RIVER ...

THERE'S A **BEAUTIFUL** PARK THERE WITH GREEN, SLOPING LAWNS THAT STRETCH TO THE EDGE OF TH' WATER. IT'S JUST FAR ENOUGH AWAY FROM TH' **HUSTLE** AN' **BUSTLE** OF DOWNTOWN BONEVILLE THAT THERE WOULDN'T BE ANY **DISTRACTIONS!**

PHONEY INVITED **EVERYBODY** IN TOWN -- AN' HE PROMISED **FREE FOOD** FOR ANYONE WHO SHOWED UP! PRETTY SOON, TH' PICNIC WAS TH' **TALK** OF **BONEVILLE!**

THEN TH' **BIG** DAY ARRIVED, AN' TH' **WHOLE TOWN** TURNED OUT! TH' KIDS WERE PLAYIN' UNDER TH' TREES, AN' THE WOMEN WORE SUN-BONNETS AN' FANCY DRESSES! THE PICNIC WAS OFF TO A **PERFECT START!**

THERE'S A **STATUE** IN TH' PARK OF BONEVILLE'S **FOUNDER** -- "BIG" JOHNSON BONE -- AN' SINCE MY COUSINS AN' I ARE **DESCENDANTS** OF HIS, PHONEY WANTED TO MAKE HIS ANNOUNCEMENT IN FRONT OF TH' STATUE.

...AND JUST TO **ADD** TO TH' FESTIVITIES, PHONEY HAD A **50**ft. **BALLOON** MADE OF HIMSELF! TH' BALLOON WAS TIED TO OL' "BIG" **JOHNSON!**

FASTEN THAT END THERE, WOULD YOU, BONE?

EVERYTHING WAS GOIN' **GREAT!** FOLKS WERE LISTENIN' TO TH' **FIRE-HOUSE** BAND AN' ENJOYIN' TH' SUNSHINE! TH' FOOD WAS PASSED OUT AN' THERE WERE PLENTY OF **PRUNE TARTS** FOR **EVERYONE!**

PRUNE TARTS?

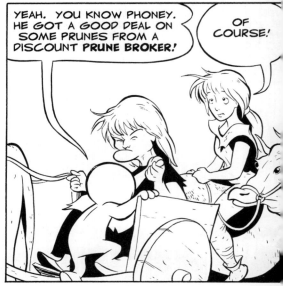

YEAH. YOU KNOW PHONEY. HE GOT A **GOOD** DEAL ON SOME PRUNES FROM A DISCOUNT **PRUNE BROKER!**

OF COURSE!

SO ANYWAY, HE MAKES THE **ANNOUNCEMENT**, RIGHT? HE GETS UP AND DECLARES HIS CANDIDACY FOR MAYOR OF **BONEVILLE!**

I STILL THINK **THAT'S** WHEN THEY SHOULD'VE RUN HIM OUT!

THAT'S WHEN A GUST OF WIND CAME OFF TH' **RIVER** AND PULLED TH' **BALLOON** LOOSE! THE STATUE CAME OFF ITS **BASE** AN' WAS DANGLIN' OFF TH' **BALLOON'S ANKLE!** ALL OF A **SUDDEN,** THIS GIANT, INFLATABLE PHONEY BONE STARTED MOVING TOWARD THE **CROWD!**

OH, MY!

YEAH, IT WAS **AMAZING!** MY FIRST-GRADE TEACHER, **MISS CRAB-BONE,** WAS THE FIRST TO **PANIC!** SHE STARTED SCREAMING AND RUNNING BACK AN' FORTH! THE BALLOON CHASED HER INTO TH' **RIVER** BEFORE SMILEY AND I COULD LET THE **AIR** OUT OF IT!

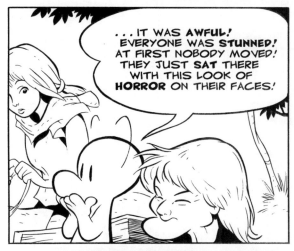

...IT WAS AWFUL! EVERYONE WAS **STUNNED!** AT FIRST NOBODY MOVED! THEY JUST **SAT** THERE WITH THIS LOOK OF **HORROR** ON THEIR FACES!

AN' **THAT'S** WHEN THEY RAN YOU OUTTA TOWN.

NO. THAT'S WHEN TH' **BAD PRUNES** KICKED IN...

. . . I JUST WANT YOU TO **KNOW** . . . I'VE BEEN **WORKING** ON **THE PLAN!** I BEEN SPREADIN' **RUMORS** ALL DAY THAT GRAN'MA BEN IS **TOO OLD** TO WIN TH' RACE THIS YEAR!

IS ANYBODY **BUYIN'** IT?

I'M TH' **BARTENDER!** THEY **GOTTA** BELIEVE ME!

THIS IS **TOO EASY!** WE'LL COVER ALL TH' **BETS,** AND THEN WHEN GRAN'MA **WINS,** WE'LL BE **RICH!**

OF COURSE, WHEN GRAN'MA GETS INTO **TOWN,** EVERYBODY'S GONNA **SEE** SHE'S PERFECTLY FIT!

I'VE GOT THAT COVERED WITH PHASE **TWO:**

THE MYSTERY COW!

A **COW** THAT WE'LL **BUILD UP** IN EVERYBODY'S IMAGINATION THAT **CAN'T** BE BEAT!

WAIT! IS **THAT** TH' PART WHERE I GET TO WEAR TH' **COW SUIT?!** OH, **JOY!**

YEAH, **THAT'S** TH' PART! BUT YOU'RE GONNA **THROW** TH' RACE! REMEMBER! WE **WANT** GRAN'MA BEN TO **WIN.**

WELL, **NATURALLY,** I'M LOOKING FORWARD TO WEARIN' A **COW SUIT** -- BUT WHAT DO **YOU** GET OUT OF IT? AFTER **ALL,** THE LOCALS DON'T USE **MONEY!** THEY TRADE GOODS 'N' SERVICES!

IT **DOES** SOUR MY PLANS FOR AMASSING A **HUGE** FORTUNE AND RETURNING TO BONEVILLE IN **TRIUMPH** . . . **STILL,** THE PLAY IS TH' THING!

IF ALL THESE YOKELS **HAVE** ARE **POULTRY PRODUCTS,** THEN I'LL **TAKE IT!!**

BESIDES, I HAVE A **HANKERIN'** TO TAKE TH' PROPRIETOR OF THIS FINE ESTABLISHMENT TO TH' **CLEANERS!** YOU **WITH** ME?

SURE! IT DOESN'T MAKE ANY DIFFERENCE TO **ME!** BUT THEN ... NOT MUCH **DOES!**

GOOD. NOW GET BACK OUT THERE AND KEEP SPREADIN' **RUMORS!**

AN' QUIT BRINGIN' ME DIRTY DISHES TO WASH!

PHONCIBLE P. BONE..... AT **LAST** I HAVE FOUND YOU.....

WHO, ME? HOW DO YOU KNOW MY NAME?

...YOU SHOULD BE GRATEFUL INDEED THAT YOUR FRIENDS INTERFERED ON YOUR BEHALF LAST NIGHT.... I AM FORCED TO USE MUCH MORE SUBTLE METHODS OF CONTACTING YOU....

WHAT TH' **HECK** ARE YOU **TALKIN'** ABOUT?

.... YOUR COUSIN FONE BONE HAS AWAKENED THE GREAT RED DRAGON..... .... FOR THIS... ... I WILL **KILL** HIM.....

133

... SO THERE HE IS, OKAY? ISHMAEL'S LAYIN' IN HIS BUNK WAITIN' FOR HIS MYSTERIOUS NEW ROOMMATE TO SHOW UP ... SUDDENLY -- AT LIKE, 3 O' CLOCK IN TH' MORNING -- TH' DOOR SWINGS OPEN ... AN' THERE, STANDIN' IN TH' DOORWAY, WITH TH' LIGHT FROM TH' HALL BEHIND HIM, IS QUEEQUEG! AN' HE'S CARRYIN' SHRUNKEN HEADS!!

WHAT'S GOING ON, BACK THERE?

OH ... H'LO, THORN.

ARE YOU TALKING ABOUT MOBY DICK AGAIN?

IT JUST SO HAPPENS THAT GRAN'MA LIKES TO HEAR ABOUT GOOD BOOKS! SHE APPRECIATES FINE LITERATURE!

HEY, GRAN'MA! WAKE UP!

ZZ--SNORT!

WHA -- ARE WE THERE ALREADY?

DOO-OOP!

NOT QUITE. BUT I THOUGHT I SHOULD WAKE YOU UP.

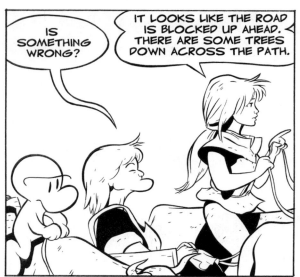

IS SOMETHING WRONG?

IT LOOKS LIKE THE ROAD IS BLOCKED UP AHEAD. THERE ARE SOME TREES DOWN ACROSS THE PATH.

STOP TH' COWS.

HMM.

THERE'S A MAN STANDING UNDER THE TREES JUST OFF TO THE SIDE OF THE ROAD. YOU SEE THAT?

WELL, I'LL BE! THAT LOOKS LIKE LITTLE JONATHAN OAKS! LET'S FIND OUT WHAT HE'S UP TO! ✳KIK✳ KIK✳ LET'S GO, COW!

GOOD AFTERNOON, JON OAKS! WHAT IN TH' WORLD ARE YOU DOIN'? WHY ARE THESE TREES BLOCKIN' TH' ROAD?

GOOD DAY, GRAN'MA BEN! LUCIUS HAD US BLOCK TH' ROAD! THERE WAS SOME STRANGE DOIN'S IN TH' WOODS LAST NIGHT. TH' HAIRY MEN WERE OUT!

YES. WE SAW THEM MAY WE PASS?

OH, YES, MA'M! COME AROUND TH' END, HERE!

H'LO, MISS THORN!

HELLO, JOHN.

GOOD LUCK WITH TH' BIG RACE, GRAN'MA! EVERYONE'S BETTIN' ON YA!

THANK YOU, DEAR!

THORN?

YES, FONE BONE?

I WANT TO THANK YOU FOR STICKIN' WITH ME LAST NIGHT . . . I DON'T KNOW WHY THOSE RAT CREATURES WERE AFTER ME -- BUT THEY WOULD'VE GOT ME FOR SURE IF YOU HADN'T STOOD UP TO 'EM!

OF **COURSE** WE STUCK TOGETHER! WE'RE FRIENDS, AREN'T WE?

HURRY UP, NOW, KIDS! WE'RE HERE!

WHERE'S **PHONEY**?

HE'S RIGHT INSIDE! I'LL CALL HIM OUT!

NOW, JUST A MINUTE! I DON'T WANT **EVERYBODY** OUT HERE! WHO'LL TAKE CARE OF TH' **CUSTOMERS**?

ET 'EM GO, .UCIUS! THESE BOYS HAVEN'T BEEN TOGETHER FOR MONTHS!

THOSE BOYS OWE ME A LOTTA **EGGS**, ROSIE . . . .

OH, ALL RIGHT . . . **CALL** HIM OUT! BUT THEN **GET BACK TO WORK!**

THANKS, YA BIG LUG!

HEY, **PHONEY!** C'MON OUT! **FONE BONE'S** HERE!

ACKNOWLEDGEMENTS

The Bone cousins managed to garner a few friends during their first year. Below the people without whose help, support, and subsequent friendship, the journey would have been very long indeed.... Larry Marder, Dave Sim, Wayne Markley, Mark Askwith, Charles Vess, and Will Eisner.

And a special acknowledgement to the animators at Character Builders, Inc; because without *them*, the journey would have been impossible: Jim Kammerud, Martin Fuller, Dan Root, and Brian Smith... the best friends an editorless cartoonist could ever want.